Dear Parent:

Congratulations! Your child is taking the first steps on an exciting journey. The destination? Independent reading!

STEP INTO READING® will help your child get there. The program offers five steps to reading success. Each step includes fun stories and colorful art. There are also Step into Reading Sticker Books, Step into Reading Math Readers, Step into Reading Phonics Readers, Step into Reading Write-In Readers, and Step into Reading Phonics Boxed Sets—a complete literacy program with something for every child.

Learning to Read, Step by Step!

Ready to Read   Preschool–Kindergarten
• big type and easy words • rhyme and rhythm • picture clues
For children who know the alphabet and are eager to begin reading.

Reading with Help   Preschool–Grade 1
• basic vocabulary • short sentences • simple stories
For children who recognize familiar words and sound out new words with help.

Reading on Your Own   Grades 1–3
• engaging characters • easy-to-follow plots • popular topics
For children who are ready to read on their own.

Reading Paragraphs   Grades 2–3
• challenging vocabulary • short paragraphs • exciting stories
For newly independent readers who read simple sentences with confidence.

Ready for Chapters   Grades 2–4
• chapters • longer paragraphs • full-color art
For children who want to take the plunge into chapter books but still like colorful pictures.

STEP INTO READING® is designed to give every child a successful reading experience. The grade levels are only guides. Children can progress through the steps at their own speed, developing confidence in their reading, no matter what their grade.

Remember, a lifetime love of reading starts with a single step!

Step into Reading, Random House, and the Random House colophon are registered trademarks
of Random House, Inc.

Visit us on the Web!
StepIntoReading.com
randomhouse.com/kids

Educators and librarians, for a variety of teaching tools, visit us at RHTeachersLibrarians.com

ISBN 978-0-449-81896-1 (trade) — ISBN 978-0-449-81897-8 (lib. bdg.)
Printed in the United States of America
10 9 8 7 6 5 4 3 2

STEP INTO READING®

STEP 1

BIG TRUCK SHOW!

By Mary Tillworth

Based on the teleplay
"Humunga-Truck!"
by Rodney Stringfellow

Based on the TV series *Bubble Guppies,*
created by Robert Scull and Jonny Belt

Cover illustrated by Sue DiCicco and Steve Talkowski
Interior illustrated by MJ Illustrations

Random House 🏠 New York

Honk, honk!
Beep, beep!
Here come
the trucks!

A fire truck is red.

It has a ladder.

The siren flashes.

The siren is loud!

A dump truck
is full of sand.
The back goes up.
The sand slides out!

9

A garbage truck
takes trash away.
Pee-yew!

Gil and Molly
hold their noses!

A mail truck
brings mail.

Goby gets a letter!

Jingle, jingle!
Here comes
the ice cream truck!

Deema eats
a sweet treat.

Oona and Nonny
drive a bread truck.

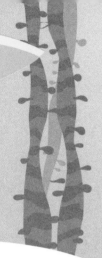

Bump!
The truck
gets a flat tire.

Oona fixes
the flat tire.

The bread truck
will soon be back
and on a roll!

It is time
for the big truck show!

The crowd
claps and cheers.

There are big trucks.

There are little trucks.

They are very

helpful trucks!

Humunga-Truck
comes out.
It is really big!

Uh-oh!

The big truck

is stuck

in the mud!

Zoom, zoom!
Here comes
the tow truck!

The tow truck hooks the big truck.

It pulls the big truck
out of the mud!

Hooray for trucks!

Hooray for

Humunga-Truck!